Welcome to the Adventures
of

Corey's Courtroom.

Will everyone please rise!

James Otis Harris
Illustrations by
Danh Tran Art

DADIELTE PRODUCTION 2017
Moreno Valley, CA.

ISBN- 978-0-9799273-0-0
LCCN 2017955850

Published and distributed by
Dadielte Production
P.O. Box 1266
Moreno Valley, CA 92556-1266

First Printing
Cover design by Danh Tran Art

Here's what kids and adults have to say to

James Otis Harris, author of

Corey's Courtroom series:

"I like how long it kept me in the story and gave great morals and values."   - Taleyna H

"Corey needs to be read in the classroom."-Connie E

"It was like I was in the courtroom listening and could see it happening."   - Kyle S

"Corey's stories are whimsical, thought provoking, entertaining and relevant." - Mona S

"Corey's stories are fun to read while giving the reader something to think about." - Willie M.

"Corey's Courtroom is an allegory emphasizing positive values and told in a way young people can easily relate."   -   Anna C.

Look for these stories by James Otis Harris!

"Corey's Courtroom"

"It's not funny to no-money bunny"

"You don't have to blend in to fit in"

"Color match"

"From Zero to Hero"

"Treating one equally is the key"

"I don't need math to have a blast"

"Sleeping ears are not as they appear"

"Temporary Care can be fair"

"I'm not a guest or a pest"

"Farm to Farm"

"Failing to share shows you don't care"

"Ditching class to fish for bass"

"Jury Duty"

Dedication:

This book is dedicated to my wonderful wife Mary whose love and support throughout the years have allowed Corey to come to life. To my children Tre and Lauren who I saw the imagination of Corey in each of them.

Introduction:

While most 7-year-olds are learning to rollerblade, Corey spends his days imagining being a judge like his father. Having his own courtroom would be a dream come true. But How?

At first, he was discouraged but then he had an idea. He could imagine the family barn as his own courtroom. The farm animals could tell him their stories and he could tell them who should say I'm sorry.

Corey cut a hole in the middle of an old blue superhero cape which became his robe. An old milk crate will be his desk and a large wooden spoon would be his gravel.

Now, when Corey closes his eyes and uses his vast imagination, the barn magically transforms into his courtroom. These are the adventures of Corey and his barnyard friends.

Welcome to Corey's Courtroom. Will everyone please rise!

Table of contents

Taking someone's test is not for the best

Today was Corey's birthday. His father promised to take him to get his favorite ice cream, double chocolate fudge after work. Corey knew he was going to hear a few cases today and could not wait to get started.

When Corey picked up Sebastian his magic spoon, it began to sing:

"Bring your problems to Judge Corey, no matter the size. Welcome to Corey's courtroom. Will everyone please rise."

"Bailiff Ben, who are we seeing today?"

"Mr. Billy Goatee, the 2nd grade history teacher."

Corey has known him for years. He's a large tall goat with round glasses sitting on the edge of his nose. They look like they are about to fall

9

off when he bends forward. His long white beard matches the few white strains of hair on top of his bald head. A piece of straw hangs from his mouth when he speaks. Corey knew he was a good teacher. "Good morning, Mr. Goatee. How can I help you today?"

"Your honor, yesterday's test assignment was to write in your own words the history of the barnyard and turn it in today. Well, Fancy Fox and Sheldon the Shetland pony turned in their papers. As I was grading I noticed Fancy's and Sheldon's papers were written in the same handwriting. You see, Fancy uses little loops and Sheldon uses big loops because of his hoofs."

"Both papers had little loops. I asked Fancy if she wrote Sheldon's paper and she said "yes". I brought Fancy and Sheldon to see you about this."

Corey could barely see Fancy's face above the desk. She was standing with her paws folded in front of her. Fancy was a small cute little girl fox. She wore blue overalls with a yellow flower on the chest pocket. Her overalls stopped at her

knees where her pink and yellow striped socks began. Her red hair was in two ponytails split right down the middle. Her blue eyes were wide open when Corey asked why she wrote Sheldon's paper for him.

"Well your Honor, Sheldon is wonderful! He is so handsome with his long black mane of hair and his shiny white teeth. He is so strong and fast, and everyone in the barnyard loves him. I even have a picture of him hanging in my locker with hearts around it.

"Today is the biggest race of the year against the other barnyards. Sheldon is our hero. He asked me to help him win the big race tomorrow. I asked, "How"? I would do anything to help the barnyard win. He said, since he needed rest for the big race he didn't have time to write his paper. He asked me if I could write it for him this one time so he could rest.

"I didn't think one time would hurt. After all, it was for the benefit of the barnyard. When Mr. Goatee found out, he gave us both bad grades and told us to re-write our papers. Mr. Goatee is making a big deal out of nothing."

Corey asked Sheldon to step forward. Sheldon was the best runner in the barnyard and a little cocky. Sheldon was wearing his blue and yellow school uniform for the race. Sheldon's legs were short for a pony but could outrun the best. That may be because his stomach was so close to the ground. Sheldon stepped forward with his head down looking up at Corey.

"Did you have Fancy write your paper so you could run in the big race?"

"Correction your Honor, so I could win the big race," he started to laugh. Corey didn't find that funny.

"Your Honor, for years we have lost the race to the other barnyards. This was finally our chance to win! There's nobody faster than me. Mr. Goatee is always giving us homework a day before a race. He could have made an exception this once. Because I had to re-write my paper I missed the race and we lost again. I hope Mr. Goatee is happy."

Corey asked the bailiff to hand him his Barnyard Book of Rules. This large heavy blue book helps Corey decide who should say I'm sorry in each case. However, this is no ordinary book, because it speaks. Corey says, "This sounds like a case of Cheating to Rest to be the Best." The book begins to rise like a cake and then shrinks back to its normal size. It opens to a light green and orange page with a few little Ts in the corner. The book begins to rhyme:

"Taking someone's test will not make them the best. To achieve any feat, you must not cheat."

Corey asked Fancy to step forward. Fancy started to feel sad. She said, "Your Honor, I wasn't trying to do anything wrong. All I wanted to do was to help us win."

Corey smiled. "What you did was wrong when you wrote Sheldon's paper. You should never do someone else's work. Even if it means you may lose a race."

Sheldon was hoping Corey wouldn't call him but he did. "Sheldon, step forward. Winning a race is not worth cheating on a test or asking someone to help you cheat. I'm disappointed in you."

"Your honor, I should not have asked Fancy to write my paper."

Corey said, "Therefore I rule that Fancy and Sheldon must apologize to Mr. Goatee for cheating. Also for the rest of the week both of you must clean the chalkboard after school."

Fancy and Sheldon turned to Mr. Goatee who was sitting in the audience next to the other animals. "We're sorry for cheating, Mr. Goatee."

Fancy hopped on Sheldon's back as they galloped around the courtroom saying, "Next year we're going to win the big race," and left the courtroom.

Corey said, "The moral of this case is: you should never cheat to win, you will lose in the end."

Before Corey father came he ask Ben, "Who are we seeing next?" Ben said, "A family from the pond." Corey wondered who that could be.

Pier Pressure

After his ice cream break with his father, Corey looked over the animals that lined his courtroom. It was time to begin. Corey bangs his magic spoon on the milk crate, and it began to sing.

"Bring your problems to Judge Corey no matter the size. Welcome to Corey's courtroom. Will everyone please rise!"

The animals stood as the song echoed around the barn. Corey was curious as to which family from the pond was here to see him. Bailiff Ben told Corey, "Mr. & Mrs. Waddle are here with their son Gus."

Corey called in the family. Mr. and Mrs. Waddle rocked from side to side as they entered the courtroom. Mr. Waddle wore a long lavender tie with white polka dots that

hung from his neck. Mrs. Waddle wore a straw hat with purple and pink flowers on it. The Waddle family has always been nice. Their children were never in trouble. Corey wondered why they were here. Corey asked Mr. and Mrs. Waddle, "What brings you to my court today?"

Mr. Waddle spoke first, "Good morning, your Honor," with a quack; his broad smile stretched across his face.

"Over the last few weeks the Missis and I have noticed Gus acting funny. He began hanging around kids called the Gliders. They are named the Gliders because when they swim, they glide real smooth across the lake. They are known to be trouble on the pond.

"Yesterday, I saw Gus and the Gliders standing on the edge of the pier. They were going to dive into the lake. This is usually no big deal, but in the late afternoon, it can be dangerous. You see, you can't see the huge black rocks from the pier after 4:00. Since kids have been hurt diving off the pier, Sheriff Croc posted no diving signs after 4:00 around the lake.

"We told Gus about diving off the pier with his new friends. He just folded his wings and frowned his face. He uttered under his breath, 'I guess I'll never have any friends and ran to his room. Two days later we received a call from Dr. Dane telling us Gus had broken his wing from jumping off the pier! Gus doesn't think he did anything wrong. So we brought Gus to see you today."

Corey remembered the Gliders. They had been in his courtroom two days earlier for jumping off the pier. Corey stared at Gus. Gus felt his stomach hurt like the time he ate three mouthfuls of candy real fast.

Corey asked, "What do you have to say about this?"

His parents called him Gus, but everyone on the barnyard called him little G. His neck was short, his wings small and his beak tiny. He often wondered when he would grow.

"Well, your Honor, I like the Gliders. They're cool! I know they're a few years older than me, but they let me hang around with them. My old

23

pals on the pond are boring. The Gliders aren't so bad, your Honor, you just don't know them."

Corey asked, "How did you hurt your wing?"

."I was standing on the pier with the gliders. The leader told me if I wanted to hang with the big Gliders I would have to pass a test. The guys said I had to jump into Lake Whatcha doing at 4:30 in the afternoon. This was my chance to be one of the guys.

"I told them what my parents said about diving into the lake after dark. The leader of the Gliders said, 'Do you always do what your parents say? Those No Diving signs are for those who are scared. If you want to be a part of us, you have to jump or go home.'

"I wanted to be part of the Gliders, so I jumped. When I looked down, I didn't see any rocks, but after I hit the water I felt my wing hurting. The Gliders just ran away when they saw I was hurt. Some of my old friends from class helped me out of the water and took me to the barnyard hospital. The doctor told me I had broken my wing."

Corey glanced around the courtroom before looking at Gus. He said, "This sounds like a case of Peer Pressure." Corey opened his Barnyard Book of Rules and asked, "What is Peer Pressure?"

The book hopped around the desk and stopped in front of Corey. It opened to an orange page with the fancy white "P" in the corner. It speaks,

"When Peer Pressure the test, don't follow the rest. When it's all said and done, a true friend won't run."

Corey leaned forward and said, "Gus, you should have listened to your parents. Peer pressure from the Gliders caused you to jump off the pier and break your wing. Your true friends are the ones who helped you to the hospital, not the ones who ran."

"I rule this is a case of Peer Pressure, and Gus, you must tell your parents you are sorry for not listening to them. You are not allowed to go to the pier for a week."

Gus turned to his parents with his broken wing in a green and red sling and told them he

was sorry for not listening. The family hugged and waddled out of the barn together.

Corey faced the animals and said, "The moral of this case is: your friends are the ones who help you out of trouble, not the ones who help you find it."

Corey saw two shadows at the barnyard door. Coming around the corner was his best friends Doc and Will. This was perfect timing because Corey looked around the barn and saw Malcolm mouse waiting to see him next.

Corey thought to himself, 'Not again, Malcolm. He took a deep breath and said, "This case will have to wait until tomorrow."

Corey hit his spoon on the desk and said, "Court's adjourned. See you tomorrow."

28

Friendship will be your pay

All the barnyard animals wanted to see why Malcolm was in court this morning. Pudgy was coming through the barn door as they were still rushing to find seats when Corey banged his spoon on the milk crate.

Bailiff Ben shouted, "Bring your problems to Judge Corey no matter the size. Welcome to Corey's courtroom. Will everyone please rise!"

Ben forgot who was coming today but remembered he wrote it on the inside of his paw. Bailiff Ben told Corey, Your Honor. Pudgy Pig couldn't wait to see you."

Corey said, "Okay, let's see Pudgy."

Pudgy was the youngest of three children of Mrs. Chubby Pig. Not only was Pudgy the youngest, but he was also the largest young pig on the farm. With a round nose and crooked smile, he was always in a good mood. Pudgy

entered the courtroom wearing his blue baseball cap backwards. His blue with the white striped T-shirt was a little too short for his tummy.

When Pudgy walked into court, Corey could see his belly-button rise above his belt buckle. His orange and blue sneakers with the green laces were untied. Corey giggled as Pudgy marched towards him, but Pudgy was not smiling. Corey pushed his spoon to the side of the milk crate and asked, "What can I do for you today, Pudgy?"

Pudgy noticed Malcolm the house mouse laughing when he was asked to speak.

Pudgy said, "All day long, Malcolm and his pals tease me. When I get on a toy, they joke about my weight and shove me out the way. During lunch they push me out of line and say, 'Don't eat everything in the barn cafeteria, save something for somebody else.' It doesn't matter if I'm on the farm playground, in class, or on my way home Malcolm and his friends pick on me because of my weight.

"Your Honor, I'm not over weight. I'm a pig! I'm supposed to be big. Anyway, I like Malcolm.

I want him to like me too. I thought if I laughed when he teased me, they would leave me alone and be my friend. But that did not work. It made things worse! But I never told them to stop."

Pudgy looked at Judge Corey with tears in his eyes. "I was embarrassed to say anything. I can't take it anymore, your Honor. So I brought Malcolm here. Maybe you can help me tell Malcolm to stop."

Corey could not believe this was happening in the barnyard. He adjusted his chair to see Malcolm better. Malcolm was always seen running from person to person teasing them. Corey also knew Malcolm was the class clown; he made everyone laugh. He was even sent to Principle Porcupine's office one morning for laughing too much in class.

Malcolm wore a red and white checkered vest with lime green headphones around his mouse ears to court. His black shorts matched his red and black high-top sneakers. Malcolm always had a lot of barnyard friends.

Corey took a drink of water and looked down at Malcolm. "Is it true that you and your friends make fun of Pudgy?"

Malcolm started looking around the barn because he knew he was in trouble.

"Come on, your Honor. I didn't think I was hurting Pudgy's feelings. We were just joking around. Pudgy would laugh when we joked about his weight. Sometimes Pudgy makes fun of himself. Is that someone who acts like he's embarrassed? Besides, he never said anything to us that something was wrong. He's too sensitive."

Corey thinks to himself, "Humm.... let me check my Barnyard Book of Rules." Corey says this sounds like a case of Bullying.

The Barnyard Book of Rule twirls and turns, then opens to a bright yellow page with a fancy brown "B" in the corner. It speaks in a low deep voice.

"Bullying to get your way will make your friends not want to stay. Always be nice in what you say, a friend for life will be your pay"

Corey asked, "Do both of you know what bullying is?"

They both stuck their tongues out at each other, shrugged their shoulders, and shook their heads "No."

Corey scooted to the front of his chair to explain. He looked down from his desk to see Pudgy's and Malcolm's face.

Corey explained, "Malcolm, you and your friends were very unkind by telling jokes about his weight. It made Pudgy feel bad about himself.

"You and your friends were bullying Pudgy to get to the front of the lunch line or to get the toys first. You even bullied Pudgy on his way home about his size. I rule that Malcolm should perform community service in the barnyard by teaching others not to bully, and apologize and to Pudgy for your behavior."

Malcolm turned and looked at Pudgy with his head down and said, "I'm sorry for joking about your weight. I didn't think what I was doing was bullying, but it was. I didn't know it made you

feel bad. I want us to be friends if that's alright with you."

Pudgy and Malcolm slapped a high five and left the courtroom together. The farm animals were ready to leave the courtroom for their afternoon snack.

But before they left, Corey said, "The moral of the story is when someone is making you feel bad even if you think they are your friends, you must tell them, "Be nice in what you say, my friendship will be your pay."

Corey heard his mother calling him for lunch. Before he left, he looked at his blackboard and could not believe who was involved in the next case.

Stealing is not appealing

After lunch, the country doctor come by Corey's house to give him his yearly flu shot. His arm was still sore when he opened the barn door.

As he entered, Bailiff Ben shouted, "Bring your problems to Judge Corey, no matter the size. Welcome to Corey's Courtroom. Will everybody please rise!"

Corey spun in his chair to see Tripp, the barnyard's patrol officer and Howie Hound sitting in his courtroom. Corey asked both of them to come to his desk.

Tripp walked slowly as Howie ran to get there first. Corey noticed Tripp had a picture in his paw.

Tripp is a large black bear with huge paws and a police hat to match. His chest is so big it makes his officer's badge look like a tiny gold speck on

his shirt. He talks like he has been in the country all his life. Tripp makes sure no trouble comes to the farm.

The farm animals call him the barnyard brass because his large brass belt buckle sparkles when he walks. The enormous buckle helps to hold up his oversized pants. Tripp was known to stumble from time to time because of his rather large grizzly bear feet.

Corey said, "Tripp, it's good to see you. How are things in the barnyard?"

"Well, your honor, I have something to show you." Tripp handed Corey a picture. "Yesterday during lunch, I saw Howie grab a bone from the barnyard cafeteria. He smuggled the bone into his backpack and left the lunchroom. I followed him to the playground. He buried the bone under the slide. That's the picture of him burying the bone now, your Honor."

"When Howie saw me take his picture, he was surprised and tried to deny he took the bone. But then he dropped his eyes, ears, and dug it

up. To my shock, when he removed the dirt, there were over a dozen bones he had buried. That Howie is a slick one."

"Corey asked Tripp, "Did you see Howie take all those bones?"

Tripp, embarrassed, started looking around. "Well, um, your Honor, he must have taken all those bones when I was on break, yeah, when I was on break."

Corey snickered because he knew Tripp sometimes falls asleep while on duty.

"Your Honor, I wanted Howie to explain why he took all those bones from the farm cafeteria. That's why we are here."

Corey turned to Howie. He knew he was new to the barnyard. Because of Howie's hefty size, he had to lean back in his chair to see him. Howie was smiling as if nothing was wrong. Corey wanted to smile back but held his grin.

"Howie, tell me about those bones buried under the slide."

Howie began wagging his furry tail like it was sweeping the floor. Howie was a tall, hairy, burley happy-go-lucky brown Labrador retriever. He wore a bright red hankie around his neck with a white 'H' stitched on it. When Howie smiled, you could see his long, pink tongue hang from one side of his mouth between his large white teeth. You could tell whenever Howie was in trouble because he smiled too much. He also had a reputation for being a little sneaky.

Corey remembered the time his father put him on time-out for taking something that was not his. He was curious to hear what Howie had to say.

"Well, your honor, as you can see, I'm big for my age. Between classes, I need a little snack until I can get home for dinner. Sometimes I take an extra bone from the lunch line and bury it under the slide. Just in case I feel hungry," Howie chuckled.

"Besides, I don't do it every day. Gee whiz, doesn't the barnyard brass have anything better to do then to take pictures of a hungry kid?" Howie started to laugh.

44

The animals listening in the courtroom started laughing as well. They began to shout, "He was just hungry. He didn't do anything wrong!"

Corey hit his spoon on the crate. "Order in the court."

Corey stood and fixed his robe. He walked over to Tripp and Howie. He looked at them while holding his chin and said, "This sounds like a case of 'Stealing is not appealing'."

At that moment, the Barnyard Book of Rules flew off the desk and into his hands. It began to rhyme:

"Stealing is not appealing, not even for a snack. Taking what's not yours shows the respect you lack."

Corey walked back to his seat. "Howie, you showed a lack of respect for the rules by taking what wasn't yours. If you're hungry, put something extra in your backpack for lunch.

"Therefore, I rule that Howie should work in the barnyard cafeteria during his lunch to pay for the bones he took and say sorry to Tripp for stealing."

Corey giggled when he heard Howie's stomach growl. He smiled but did not say anything.

Howie said, "I'm sorry, Mr. Tripp, for stealing bones. Based on what the Barnyard Book of Rules said about stealing, I understand now that stealing for any reason is wrong."

Tripp overheard Howie's stomach growl too and handed him a chocolate-covered bone for later. When Howie saw the bone, his eyes widened and his mouth began to water. As they were leaving the court, Tripp fell over a bale of hay. Tripp and Corey along with all the animals laughed as they left the courtroom.

When the courtroom closed for the day. Corey said, "The moral of this case is: It doesn't matter if you steal for a friend, for a toy or a snack. Stealing is wrong and that's a fact."

Corey said, "Courts adjourned"!

As Ben started sweeping the barn, Corey's sister wanted him to play with her before dark. As he left the barn, he saw Hanna Hen

and Choo-Choo chicken standing by the door.
They were not happy, but why?

The Golden Pie Lie

Corey loved the barnyards county fair. Every fall the best Corn-Cob Pie makers would gather together to win the Golden Pie award. Corey heard Choo-Choo had won for the first time this year.

Bailiff Ben started to say "Bring your..." but Corey stopped him.

Corey asked, "Ben, do you mind if I say it this time?"

Ben smiled and said, "Okay."

Corey stood on his milk crate with his arms in the air and said in a high-pitched voice, "Bring your problems to Judge Corey, no matter the size. Welcome to Corey's Courtroom. Will everyone please rise!"

Corey chuckled to himself and said, "It sounds better when you say it. Who are we seeing today?".

50

"Hanna Hen and Choo-Choo Chicken," said Bailiff Ben.

Corey said, "Choo-Choo the winner of this year's contest? Why is she here? Okay, bring them in."

Corey knew Hanna and Choo-Choo had been bitter rivals in the annual pie baking contest. Whoever won was guaranteed to sell the most pies that year. Hanna had won the contest for the last three years. This made Choo-Choo furious. This year Choo-Choo vowed to win at all cost.

Corey could smell the Corn-Cob Pie sitting on his desk. "Bailiff, why are the two best bakers here one day after the competition?"

"Hanna claims Choo-Choo did not win fair and square."

Corey raised his eyebrows and said, "Is that true, Hanna?

Hanna stepped to the milk crate. Hanna was a large round hen with yellow and brown feathers with white tips. She wore a brown sun hat with white trim to court.

"Well, your Honor, cluck, cluck. As you know, yesterday was the county bake off. The best pie makers bring their Corn-Cob pie to be judged. It always comes down to me against Choo-Choo Chicken.

"Yesterday I brought my pie to the judges' booth before the contest began. A sign hung over the judges' table saying, 'You can't eat happiness but Corn-Cob pie is the next best thing.' I thought that was funny, your Honor.

"Anyways, before the judges could taste my pie, one of my chicks got sick. I had to return to the hen house for some medicine.

"By the time I came back the judging was over. Choo-Choo had won the contest. I had won the last three years, so I wasn't too upset. My thoughts were: may the best pie win.

"Everyone was eating the pie and telling Choo-Choo how wonderful it was. I was curious, so I asked my friend Howie if I could have a taste of his. After one bite, I knew this was my pie. "I was so upset; I ran back to the hen house. On my way, I found my pie tin under a bush

behind the barn. I know it was mine because I placed a giant double "H" inside the bottom of the tin. I asked Choo-Choo about it, and she said I must have been mistaken.

"Your Honor, it was my pie that won. Choo-Choo lied to the judges. She passed off my pie as hers. By the time I found out the judges were gone. I brought Choo-Choo in today to get to the truth, your Honor."

The animals were starting to enter the barn because they could smell the Corn-Cob pie. Corey asked Choo-Choo what's up.

Choo-Choo's real name is Charlotte but everyone calls her Choo-Choo because she lives in the wheel of an old train behind the barn. She was a short chicken with red and brown feathers with white tips. She wore an apron to court that said, "Pie isn't everything, but it's real close."

Choo-Choo looked at Corey and started to worry. He could see she was beginning to sweat.

"Your honor, cluck, cluck. Hanna wins every year. All I dreamed of was winning the prize. I

could not take Hanna winning again, so I switched the pies when the judges turned their heads and told them Hanna's pie was mine. I knew it was wrong when I won, but the deed had already been done. So I didn't say anything.

"I was scared, so I told Howie the hound to bury the pie tin behind the barn. But all Howie did was put it under a bush."

Choo-Choo turned and glared at Howie who was sitting in the back of the barn and said, "Good help is hard to find, your Honor."

Corey gave Choo-Choo a napkin to wipe the sweat from her forehead.

Corey said, "This sounds like a case of 'willing to lie to win a prize.'"

The Barnyard Book of Rule grows feathers and opens to a green page with a Gold "L" in the corner. It begins to rhyme,

"Whenever you tell an untruth, you're like a tree that produces rotten fruits. It doesn't matter if you win, lose or tie. It's never worth winning if you have to lie."

"Choo-Choo you lied to win the award, something that you adored. But you didn't win it honestly. Lying to win is no way to be. You had Howie help you lie when you told him to bury the pie tin. Never involve someone else in your lies.

"Therefore, I rule you must tell Hanna, the judges and Howie you're sorry for lying to win the prize. Hanna is the true winner."

Choo-Choo used the napkin from Corey to wipe off her sweat. She turned to Hanna and said, "I'm sorry for switching pies and lying to the judges."

Choo-Choo turned around and called Howie from the back where he was listening,

"Charlie, I'm sorry for dragging you into the middle of my lie. You're a nice guy."

Hanna said, "Choo-Choo, come over to the hen house tomorrow. I will help you with your pie. But I won't give you my secret recipes."

Hanna and Choo-Choo started to chuckle before they skipped out of the barn.

Corey turned to the crowd of animals that were waiting for the next case and said, "The moral of the story is a lie is a lie. It doesn't matter if it's for something as big as a contest

or as simple as a pie. Remember, having others to assist, is another lie you can't dismiss."

As Corey was eating a piece of pie he watched as Ben wrote on the blackboard the next case. There was a whisper in the courtroom about who was next. When Corey saw her, he knew it was only a matter of time.

Don't go spreading the news

This was Corey's last case of the afternoon. Bailiff Ben left a little early to go to his son's baseball game. So Corey sent word to the barnyard that he needed to find a substitute bailiff for court.

When little Benny Beaver heard the news, he swam from the pond and asked,

"Can I be bailiff for the rest of the day?" Benny always wanted to grow up and be like Ben.

Corey grinned and asked, "Do you know what to say?"

With his two white front teeth showing he said, "Do I"!

Benny grabbed a book he found on Corey's desk, and then placed it on a haystack and stood on it. He cried at the top of his lungs,

"Bring your problems to Judge Corey no matter the size. Welcome to Corey's Courtroom. Will everyone please rise!"

Corey knew the animals could barely hear him but said, "Good job. Who are we seeing today?"

Benny said, "Sissy Sparrow and Hattie Hoot Owl flew in this afternoon to talk to you."

Corey had not seen Sissy since last spring when she was a baby bird. She had grown up since then. Her feathers were bright blue and silver with a little black triangle on her neck where she wore a beautiful gold pendant. Corey saw that she was wearing blue nail polish that did not match her feathers and giggled to himself.

"Sissy, what brings you to my court today?"

Sissy flew to the front of the milk crate just to get a little closer to Corey.

"Your Honor, last week I flew by myself for the first time. You see, when we sparrows leave the nest and fly for the first time, our parents give us a big party. My party is in a few weeks. I was so excited! I was going to send out hundreds of invitations to the barnyards in the area.

"Well a few days ago at lunch. I was talking to my friend Renny Robin about the invitations. Before I could finish she told me nobody wanted to come to my party from the other farms. I asked why?

"She said Hattie overheard me say I did not want to invite our friends from the other barnyards to the party. When she heard this, she went from farm to farm telling all my friends I was not inviting them.

"I'm so upset. I thought I would bring Hattie to your courtroom today to clear up the matter."

When Corey looked at Hattie, her large round yellow eyes were wide open. She knew she was in trouble. She thought if she wore her lucky green dress with the yellow Polk-a-dots that matched her green shoes to court, it might help.

Corey asked Hattie to fly to the front of his desk.

Corey knew Hattie the owl had made a name for herself as the barnyard bigmouth. She was always meddling in everyone's business.

Whenever someone is talking she interrupts and says 'Whoo? Whoo?'"

During recess, Corey spotted Hattie sitting high in the pine trees listening to the animals talk. Sometimes Hattie would turn her head in a complete circle not to miss anything. Corey asked Hattie about what she said.

"Your Honor, I was sitting back to back at lunch with Sissy and I know what I heard. She is just mad because the other farms found out that she was not going to invite them to the party. All I did was spread the news."

Sissy flapped her feathers at Hattie and said, "You only heard half the story."

Corey said, "Go on."

"What I said was, I did not want to invite anyone from the other farms without first asking my friends from our barnyard.

"Hattie only heard half of what was said and didn't get the whole story. She blabbed to the other barnyards and they became upset. Now nobody wants to come to my party."

Corey asked Hattie, "Did you hear everything that was said?"

Hattie with her head down said, "I may have missed the last part of what Sissy said. I did leave before Sissy was finished speaking with Renny." With both wings on her hips, Hattie chuckled and said, "You know us owls are known for our sight, not our hearing," as she laughed nervously.

Corey began to look for his Barnyard Book of Rules, but couldn't find it. He asked Benny "Have you seen my book?" Benny looked around shrugged his shoulders and said "No, your Honor."

Corey looked down and saw Benny had placed the Barnyard Book of Rules on the haystack and was standing on it.

The book was coughing when Benny handed it to Corey. Corey said, "This sound like a case of Spreading half the news."

The Barnyard Book of Rule turns to stone then opens to a light green page with a yellow "S" in the corner. The book begins to rhyme.

"Don't go spreading the word over something you half heard. Get all your facts, or the knowledge you will lack."

Corey leaned forward towards Hattie and said, "Hattie, you told Sissy's other barnyard friends they were not invited. You only had half the truth. You almost ruined Sissy's party.

Therefore, I rule, Hattie should say I'm sorry to Sissy for listening to only part of the story and spreading the news."

Hattie said, "I'm sorry Sissy. From now on when I hear someone talking, I will not say who, who, but listen to everything that is said and not spread the news."

Sissy asked if Hattie would like to help her send out her invitations. Hattie said, "Great!" and flew out the barn window together.

Corey turned to the crowd of animals in the court and said, "The Moral of the story is to make sure you get the whole truth before you go telling half the news."

There was a line of animals waiting outside to see Corey. But this was his last case of the day. Just before Corey leaped from his chair to go to dinner, he hit his spoon on the milk crate and said, "Courts adjourned! See you tomorrow in Corey's Courtroom!"

Run, hide or fight
with all your might!

The farm was unusually quiet this morning when Corey entered the barn. So quiet, he heard the farm mice run to their seats. Days earlier, there had been trouble on another barnyard and everyone was nervous. Corey was told someone had spit BBs through a straw hitting some of the farm animals. Corey knew his friends were wondering what to do.

Crash was standing in the courtroom with his arms crossed when Corey entered. Crash was from the farms Classroom Emergency Response Team otherwise known as CERT. He brought Bruce the bull to court this morning. Corey knew whenever Crash was in his courtroom it was serious. He only came if he felt the barn animals were in danger.

Crash was the captain of the CERT team. He was a large grey wolf with large white paws. He wore a green and yellow uniform which had pockets everywhere. He spoke into a black radio that rested on his chest. On one side of his sleeve it said CERT in large yellow letters. When he spoke, he howled like he was howling at the moon.

"Crash, I heard you were having drills in school because there was someone shooting BBs on another barnyard. Is that true?"

Crash howled and said, "Yes, your Honor. We were told someone from the uptown farm went to school and spit BBs hitting several animals. Some had to go to the farm hospital. We here at CERT call him an active spit shooter. It has never happened here but we thought it was a good idea to have a barnyard drill just in case. We want our kids to be prepared.

"So this past week we have been practicing what to do if you hear someone shooting BBs at school. During class we taught everyone to Run, Hide or Fight. Otherwise if you hear shooting you are to run to a safe place. go hide out of sight, or be prepared to fight.

"Bruce refused to learn the three steps of 'Run Hide, or Fight' with the class. He stuck out his tongue and said, 'I know what to do in case of trouble. I will yell, shout and throw things at anyone shooting BBs at me. I'm smart, strong and tough,' while showing his muscles.

"He was shocked this morning when we held a surprise drill. Everyone knew what to do except Bruce. He didn't do anything the class practiced. When he heard the BBs being shot in the hallway and saw all the commotion, he froze and panicked. Instead of running to an exit, he ran to a corner hoping not to be seen. He didn't have an escape plan or try to run, hide or fight. Bruce caused his classmates and himself to get hit. Everyone was upset because Bruce didn't follow the three steps. After class, I escorted him to Principle Porcupine's office. We are here to see you about this, your Honor."

Corey rolled up both sleeves and said to Bruce, "Let me hear from you."

Bruce was big for his age, even for a baby bull. His blue Mohawk hairdo made him look tougher than he was. He wore a gold ring in his

nose. His red T-shirt had the sleeves torn off to show off his muscles. He didn't think he needed to follow the training because he was cool and smart.

Bruce walked up, placed his hand on Corey's desk and leaned forward with his legs crossed.

Before he could speak, Corey said, "Bruce, stand up straight in court."

Bruce grinned and stood at attention. "Your Honor, the surprise exercise wasn't fair. Crash knew I was taking a test and was not ready. He did it to make me look bad. I remember the rule: Fight, Hide or Run. No, no, I mean Hide, Fight or Run. I'm not sure, but next time I will get it right.

Corey was not smiling when he said, "this sounds like a case of: Doing it your way, may be the price others have to pay.

The Barnyard Book of Rules begins to spin like a top then stops. It speaks,

"Doing things your way will cause others to pay. The training was right. If there is an active shooter, you must Run, Hide or Fight! Be as safe as you can. Always have an escape plan."

Corey turned to Bruce and said, "Because you followed your own rules, you didn't know what to do. You caused yourself and your classmates to be hit by the shooter. You must be at your best, because someday it may not be a test. Therefore, I rule Bruce should say I'm sorry to Crash and the class for putting everyone in danger. I'm happy this was only practice.

Bruce looked with his head down and said,

"It's true I didn't know the safety rule of Run, Hide or Fight. It's important we all know what to do in an emergency. Mr. Crash, can I take the class again? I want to teach others animals the three steps and how to be safe."

Crash turned and told Bruce "Class is tomorrow at 8:00 AM sharp. Oh yeah, bring the donuts." They laughed.

Corey gave Crash a high five and told him his CERT team is doing a great job preparing the barnyard. The courtroom started to get noisy as the animals left the barn.

Corey stood holding his spoon, but before he hit his desk he said,

"The moral of the story is, if there is trouble at school, morning, noon or night. Always remember, to Run, Hide or Fight. Run to an exit and get out of sight. Do this with all your might!"

Corey's stomach began to growl. He was ready for dinner. Before he left the courtroom, he started to sing. "Bring your problems to Judge Corey, no matter the size. Welcome to Corey's Courtroom. Will everyone please rise!" Corey could not believe tomorrow's case is involving....

James is a law school graduate and a law enforcement retiree. James's book was inspired by a courthouse field trip taken way back when he was in elementary school. Corey's Courtroom is a series of fun stories using Corey's gifted imagination and farm animals to help with real world problems. The stories are designed to assist in safely resolving conflict while keeping friendships. In addition, Corey provides morals and values while developing problem-solving skills.

James resides in Southern California with his wife and is a father of two. He hopes the stories in Corey's Courtroom bring you and your child as much joy as he experienced writing them.

Welcome to Corey's Courtroom!

74824775R00044

Made in the USA
San Bernardino, CA
20 April 2018